May your life be filled with beautiful stories.

Dear ___________________________

Love & Regards

___________________________

# Have a great time!

Title: Heart-Stirring Moments
eBook/Paperback/Audio
Author: Rose Butterfly
Category: **Short stories/Feelings/Emotions**



Cover Design: Deena Philip

Illustrations
Deena Philip
Courtesy: Pixabay

**Disclaimer**
This is a work of fiction. Any resemblance to actual persons, living or dead, or actual events is purely coincidental.


**Author's email:** reach2rosebutterfly@gmail.com
www.cheerproductions.com.au

# A Short Story Collection

By Rose Butterfly

Vol. 1

# Heart-Stirring Moments

# Contents

**Also features quotes from**

**THE BOOK I NEVER HAD**

# STORY #1
# LITTLE LOVE

How can the one who abandoned you,
ever receive you again?

## Desperation. Frustration. And then silence.

And then again, I sank into that familiar, heavy sense of desperation.

I couldn't stop myself from feeling these emotions – anger, confusion, fear, and so many others. I wanted to be strong. I wanted to feel like myself again.

---

But what I didn't understand then was that healing takes time, sometimes far longer than we expect.

---

Looking back now, the most important thing isn't that I struggled or felt broken. It's that I held on. I stayed, even when it hurt so much or I could barely breathe. Even when I felt completely alone.

When I couldn't share what I was feeling, it felt like I was carrying an invisible weight, one that never loosened.

I came to my own conclusions: *"There is nothing called real love,"* I told myself over and over, convincing myself not to fall for any more traps, not to hold onto naive ideas.

But when I look back now, I see something different: I was strong because I stayed. I stayed with myself, holding everything I felt, even when it seemed impossible.

---

I stayed because I chose to. When love chose to betray me, I chose to remain. I chose to stand by someone I knew well – a girl who was kind, loving, and sincere.

---

I chose her, deliberately and fondly. I stayed for her. I stayed for me.

If I asked you, would you ever go after the one who abandoned you? Would you run after someone who walked away? Would you trust them again?

Or does your heart still ache for them, even when you know their love never truly included you?

Do you silently hope for their return, imagining life together again? Do you carry a secret hope, a longing that never quite dies, even when you know it may never happen?

Many people carry the weight of abandonment. The feeling of someone you loved and trusted leaving you behind is hard to describe.

It shatters your sense of safety and leaves you wondering if anyone can truly be trusted.

---

You may be left with a wound that never properly heals, a secret you can't share, and a half-hearted smile you wear to get through your day. There's an emptiness that feels impossible to fill.

---

You might try to fill it with friends, with new relationships, with work or hobbies but does it ever really work?

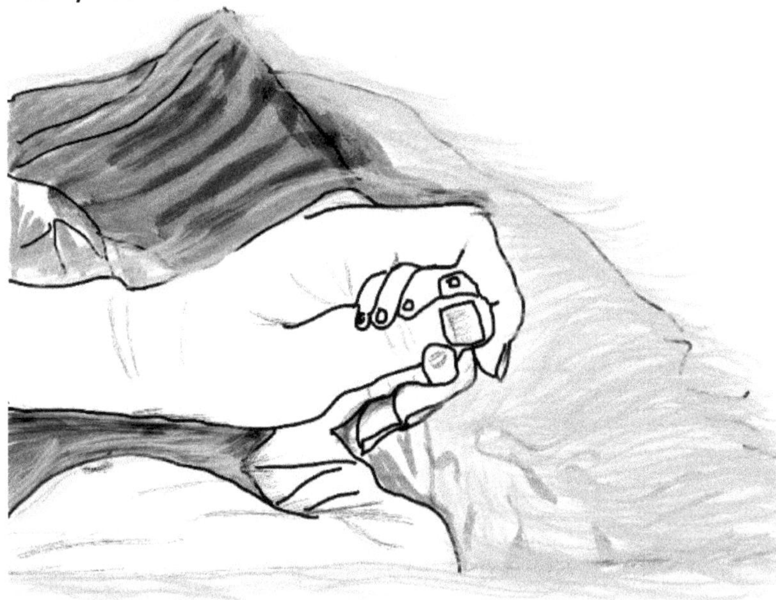

Now imagine a child being abandoned by their mother.

How does a child let go of that thought?

How do they release the memory of a love that was supposed to be unconditional?

"She is my mother," the heart insists, clinging to an idea that should have been safe and lasting.

But can a love that is abandoned ever be whole again? Is it foolish to hope for a reunion, or is it sometimes part of healing?

Should you ever go back to someone who left you behind?

> You might think that finding them would fix everything—that they would welcome you, and you would belong again, as if nothing had happened.

But you might be wrong.

The truth is people who abandon you often have no capacity to receive you again.

This is my story.

It isn't just about a mother leaving her child. It's about the moment I realised the existence of something I call little love.

What is little love?

It's a love that exists, yes, but in tiny, insufficient amounts—often found in selfish, careless hearts.

Have you ever experienced that kind of little love?

---

He held onto my hands, his grip gentle yet firm, reassuring me as we crossed the chaotic streets of Mumbai.

---

Mumbai during the rainy season can be brutal, packed with people, deafening noises, and relentless traffic.

The honking of vehicles mixes with shouting voices and the sound of heavy rain, creating a kind of chaos that presses on all your senses at once.

Especially during the monsoon, the roads turn into shallow rivers, and your legs sink into murky water with every step.

Crossing the streets at such times feels like wading through an unpredictable pool, trying to dodge people rushing past you, bikers weaving between cars, and vehicles splashing water as they speed by.

And umbrellas? Most of them are useless against the kind of rain Mumbai gets, flimsy shields that flip inside out with one strong gust of wind. People carry them anyway, perhaps for the gesture, but everyone knows they barely help.

Even in such hostile weather, life doesn't slow down. If anything, it speeds up. People rush harder, move faster.

Everyone is trying to reach somewhere, desperate not to be trapped in the downpour.

But even in that chaotic, slippery moment, I could sense the warmth of his hold.

For some, like us, the rainy season isn't all that bad. The wetness, the cold, and someone to hold—does that really sound bad to you?

I liked the rains because during those times, he was always more cautious, more protective than usual.

---

He would look around with such intensity while crossing the street, one arm instinctively covering me, making sure I was safe.

---

That's what he always did, ensured I was safe and comfortable. And there was something about his hold, it wasn't just about keeping me from slipping or shielding me from traffic. It was the kind of hold that silently said, "I will be with you forever."

You don't need too many things to know when someone truly loves you. Sometimes their presence is enough. Through their presence, they say it—through unspoken words. Their eyes communicate in ways no words could ever capture. And doesn't that mean something?

Or are we only capable of sensing what is spoken out loud now? And if it's not spoken, does it mean something entirely different?

Sometimes love doesn't need to be spoken—it's shown in these small, consistent moments. But the world doesn't always work like that, does it?

---

These days, everything has to be said out loud, promised, or even signed into a contract.

---

People want proof. Without it, silence can mean uncertainty, even indifference. That was our kind of silence. It meant different things to each of us.

For me, it meant commitment. For him, it meant something else entirely.

We always found our own space and moments to be together, somehow balancing our distinct, separate lives.

He was the only person I felt close to, outside my small family of my father and my sister. His eyes always sparkled when he looked at me, and every gesture, every word he spoke, felt like love in abundance.

That gentle love, for me, was synonymous with a mother's love, unimaginably beautiful, warm, and safe. And what could ever be greater than a mother's love?

I imagined that a mother's care and presence must feel this magical too.

I don't have any memories of my own mother. She left right after I was born, choosing her own life instead.

My father always said, "It's okay to find your way, even if it means stepping away from the people you've been with or leaving behind the ones you love."

But I never believed that. Not the harsh truth of our mother leaving us, but the idea that you shouldn't pursue those who abandon you.

---

> I always felt the three of us should have gone after her, chased her down, and confronted her.

---

She would have expected that, wouldn't she? If I were the one to ever leave, I would expect someone to come after me.

We should have followed her, stood in front of her, shown her our faces and then she would have looked at us and felt so miserable she wouldn't have been able to resist coming back.

That's what I believed would happen.

That's what real love is like, it surrounds you, grows, and fills every space.

And how do I know this?

Because I experience it every single day. I feel that secure love in his presence. Hence, the certainty.

The one thing I was absolutely sure about was that he was going to be with me forever. I always sensed that when he was around me.

Like every love story, we had our own problems, but I never thought about them. In fact, I didn't even know we had problems or that something might be wrong.

I thought our relationship was perfect, the kind of bond nobody else could understand because it felt so extraordinarily special to me.

But now I know.

---

Now I know it wasn't perfect. It wasn't that special. Something was not quite right.

---

And now I know what it was.

It was us and our silence.

We never spoke of love.

We never spoke of marriage.

We never planned. We lived as if love alone was all we would ever need.

One day, my father told us girls that we had to move to Hyderabad.

He was getting a new job, and he had to take that offer because our financial situation wasn't getting any better.

A better job with better pay meant a lot to us at that time. Living in Mumbai with what we had wasn't easy—every month felt like a stretch, a careful balancing act of expenses.

So, any better option at that point had to be considered, no matter what it cost emotionally.

---

But this move wasn't just about a new city. It meant leaving behind the place we had grown up in, the narrow streets and small markets that had shaped our childhood.

---

It also meant leaving behind something far more personal: my father's quiet expectation of his wife's return… and our own fragile hope of our mother's return.

All those years in that tiny home, we had shared a single dream, a hope that hovered in the air like something sacred.

Sometimes father would think out loud, saying, *"What if your mother comes right now, knocking on that door?"*

He would smile faintly, almost shyly, and say how he would open the door, wondering who could be there, only to be shocked and overjoyed to see her.

He would imagine how she'd look into his eyes with so much fondness and ask softly, "And you thought I could live without you?"

___

And then, like it was a little family ritual, each of us would take turns creating our own versions of that moment.

___

I would act out how she'd see me and just burst into tears—tears from seeing how tiny I had been when she left. I'd imagine her hugging me tightly, apologising, crying her heart out.

In my version, I would tell her not to cry. *"It's okay,"* I'd say, *"you're here now. You can be with us."*

My sister would add her own version, talking about how, if our mother came, she would remind her of their times together—making pretty hairstyles, drawing pictures side by side, and sharing that special bond only they seemed to have.

Whenever she said that, I would feel a strange sting in my chest, a hollow ache because I never got to know her that way.

She never touched me. She never caressed my hair or looked into my eyes with that quiet intensity that mothers are known for.

I would feel this massive weight pressing on my heart every time I realised that... but I would push it aside and join my father and sister in those crazy little moments of celebrating an imaginary return.

---

Since my sister had vivid memories of our mother, she would often imitate her subtle mannerisms, the way she spoke, the soft, tilted smile. She would show off her memory of our mother like it was a little treasure.

---

I liked that part because, in those moments, it truly felt like she was there. In fact, I had seen it so many times that I even narrated those enactments to my friends, as if I had memories of her myself.

But every now and then, I would gently remind my sister that our mother might have changed over time. *"She's probably older now,"* I would say, *"and maybe she looks very different too."*

Still, that thought of her return was slowly fading, becoming less real—overshadowed by the very real and urgent need to stabilise our finances.

Looking back, I realise how hard that decision must have been for my father. Leaving behind a memory or a hope is never easy. It's like cutting off a piece of yourself.

> Sometimes, though, leaving behind both memories and hope is necessary to move forward. That's just how life works, and when you truly realise it, it pulls you to the other side, the better side.

With our mother never around, my sister and I often grew up wondering what it would have been like if she had been there, especially during tough times—like when one of us was sick and craved that unique, tender care only mothers seem to have.

We had seen how mothers could become so deeply caring and loving toward their children during such moments, and we longed for it in silence.

And then came this new chapter, unfolding right in front of us:

**The move.**

That meant a lot. Moving from one state of residence to another is never just a physical move. It is a shift of energy, a transference of everything familiar into something unknown, while also letting a whole new energy seep into you.

When such a move happens in your life, it is not just relocation—it is transformation.

---

Keep your eyes and ears open, because sometimes, a move is a divine decision.

---

I quickly made a call to him and told him.

I was nervous, my hands slightly trembling as I held the phone, worried about how he would take the news of me having to leave Mumbai.

But deep down, I believed it would all be okay, eventually. Because he was my man.

So, I told him… and he was quiet.

That silence wasn't ordinary; it had a weight, a strange heaviness to it, a whiff of something unpleasant that immediately unsettled me.

I asked him softly, *"Will you come?"*

*"No,"* he said, his voice calm but distant.

"Obviously not immediately," I explained quickly. "You can't just leave everything and come now. But eventually you would. Right?" I asked, almost pleading.

*"No. I don't think so,"* he said again, this time firmly.

*"What?"* My mind froze. I couldn't process his words. They were coming at me, but they refused to settle inside my head. It was like my brain was actively rejecting them, refusing to comprehend.

*"I have to take care of my future,"* he said. *"I have a great job here, and I have great dreams for my future. You will have to move on with your life."*

That was not the reply I expected. In my mind, I had imagined so many different reactions from him—sadness, hesitation, maybe even anger—but never a big, definitive *never*.

What happened to me during that conversation is still blurry to this day.

I think my mind has erased parts of it, like it refuses to let me fully revisit those moments.

But one thing I do remember clearly is what I felt.

A strange emotion I had never truly accepted before, something I had never believed could happen to me.

It struck me sharply, like a sudden pinch in my heart, a sharpness that spread through my entire body.

*This is what it's like,* I thought.

Did I ever wonder what it felt like to be abandoned?

Then why am I being made to experience it so vividly? Why was I chosen to feel this?

It was a dark, heavy realisation:

**ABANDONMENT.**

Somewhere deep within me, I had sensed it before, but I had buried it. And now it came back, rushing up like something regurgitated from the past.

---

This time, I felt it fully, wrapping around me from head to toe, sinking into my skin.

---

At that moment, I felt the pain of that little child again, the child whose mother had walked away even though she was just a baby.

The pain of that tiny heart whose cries were unheard, whose mother didn't care enough to even stay long enough to see her smile or hear her first words.

She didn't care about my existence.

That pain, buried deep for years, began to grow. It spread like vines around my heart, choking me, climbing up my throat, my eyes, my face.

<hr>

It killed that sweet, innocent smile I once carried and hardened it into a frown of disbelief and despise.

<hr>

I put down the call and cried my heart out—not just for that moment but for many years after.

Many times, I thought about how my father must have felt when my mother left him.

How did he manage two girls, raising them alone, while holding back any bitterness towards our mother?

That journey must have been unbearably hard because seeing us every day must have been a constant reminder of her and, with it, a lingering ray of hope for her return.

I left Mumbai. And then, over the years, I moved to many places.

A new place, and then another, and then another… but no matter where I went, I always reached out to him.

And he always remained the same.

*"Never, I can't be with you."*

One day, I stopped asking.

---

*Maybe it's too late*, I thought. But still, it was a beginning. And beginnings are important—moments where you stop, breathe, and choose to look in a new direction, to seek what is truly intended for you.

---

This is what I want to tell you, my friend:

Never chase after those who abandoned you. They have no intention of returning.

You will have to take charge of your life.

Like I did. Like my father did.

Because there is so much love around you. Love that is real, love that stays.

But the love from someone who abandoned you?

That is an impotent love. A love that is hardly there.

**Very little... not enough.**

*Little Love* is dedicated to all of you, who had to go through abandonment from the people you least expected and the heaviness you still carry as part of what you went through.

May you be surrounded by true love, real love and may it be in abundance.

# Rose Butterfly

# STORY #2
# MEMORY

She is waiting...

## I'm not sure how long I've been standing here.

I don't even know if I was meant to be here.

Was I supposed to be somewhere else?

Why am I here at this bus stop, of all places?

There was a strange emptiness in my chest, a hollow space I couldn't explain.

> At that moment, it felt like I was in a place called *nowhere*—a place you can't describe, can't put into words, and certainly can't share with anyone else.

I stood like that for a while because I was waiting.

Did I say I was waiting?

For what exactly?

What am I waiting for?

I couldn't quite put my finger on it.

But I knew there was something that I was waiting for, even if I couldn't name it.

I held onto my six-year-old's hand firmly, grounding myself with her tiny fingers curled into mine, and decided to walk toward a large restaurant across the street. We crossed over, my steps slow and unsure, but deliberate.

Inside, the air shifted. A man greeted me at the door with a warm smile.

Did he know me? His face looked familiar, like someone I'd seen before, maybe in another time, another place.

The restaurant was beautiful. The soft yellow lights glowed warmly, the décor balanced elegance and comfort, and every table was alive with movement and chatter.

It was the kind of space that made you feel like you'd stepped into a small world that belonged entirely to itself.

People were laughing, eating, lost in their conversations, and somehow, every single one of them looked like they belonged there.

Nobody looked uncomfortable.

Nobody looked lost.

They all seemed to know why they were there, what they had come for.

Isn't that wonderful, to just know your reason for being in a moment?

---

I looked at my daughter, her eyes wide and curious, sparkling as she took it all in. She looked thrilled, and that alone made me happy.

---

Maybe the thought of sitting down in a restaurant and having a proper meal is exciting for a six-year-old.

But I had to be careful.

She couldn't run around here. If she slipped away, it would be hard for me to catch up with her in such a busy place.

So, I bent down and whispered, *"Darling, always stay with Mamma, okay?"*

*"I always stay with you,"* she replied softly, her little voice certain and warm.

I looked at her face for a moment.

I think she knew something was different today.

She could sense it. Maybe she was wondering why we were here, sitting in a place like this.

Was today special?

Was it a celebration?

Or was it just a mother-daughter adventure, one of those days where nothing is planned but everything still feels important?

I looked around at that restaurant, my eyes falling on every bit of that space.

As I observed the restaurant, I realised that there was something very familiar about the place.

I know this place, I thought. I think I have been here before. Not sure with whom though. Maybe with my mother.

I don't remember my mother too well. And also, I can't quite put my finger on when I came here.

Now that I look at this place again, I realise that I don't know this place.

*I don't think I have been here before.*

I went straight to the back of the kitchen and stood there. Nobody appeared to have noticed me, or perhaps they were too busy running around and doing their work.

---

I *caught* a glimpse of a woman in the kitchen, and my heart started to race. She looked so familiar, but I can't quite put my finger on why?

---

She looked at me with a warm smile and *asked* me if I could pass some of the dishes to her from the lower shelves.

I gave her what she had asked for. But I kept thinking how I knew her.

*Who is she? I feel an urge to scream out and ask her who she is.*

Will that be awkward? It seems like she knows me.

Then a faint memory came into my mind. I know her as a man, but that's not how he looks now.

He is very feminine, but that smile, it has the same soul. *He is a lady now.*

---

I stared in disbelief, struggling to comprehend what I was seeing. *When had he become a woman?* I vividly remember talking to him and working with him right here, in this very place.

---

She then looked at me and said, *"Why are you standing here, go to the restaurant and enjoy yourself."*

I listened to her and stepped out of the kitchen and looked at that big place full of people, talking, enjoying, having food. But what I did not understand was, *why I was there?*

I held onto my daughter, afraid to let go of her hand. I did not want to lose her in the crowd.

One thing that I know for sure is not to leave that tiny hand even when I have no clue where I am.

How can I know why I'm here? How can I figure it out? I thought to myself, my mind spinning in circles.

How did I get here? Did someone drop me off here or did I walk into this place on my own? I wish someone would tell me. I kept thinking about where I was before I came into this place.

What even is this place?

> It looks like a restaurant. Looks like I have been here before. I better act normal and not make it suspicious.

The only thing I always need to be careful about is not to let go of my sweet little Eva.

Her tiny fingers were wrapped firmly around mine, warm and soft, grounding me in that moment.

I walked to a table; they knew me—or at least they behaved like they did. They asked how I was doing. I smiled nervously and told them I was standing for the election and wanted to be on everyone's good books.

I even told them I would be visiting every table to say 'hi'. I had no intention of speaking that way, but I did. I spoke those words only because I thought I sounded smart. The words just spilled out before I could think much.

*Did I say something stupid?*

They gave me a weird, confused look, a look I couldn't quite read, and I wasn't able to judge what they meant by it. Despite not knowing, I walked up to different tables and said hi, forcing a polite smile on my face.

That's when I realised—my presence did not make any difference to anyone there. It was like I was invisible, like whatever I said or did simply did not matter.

Why would it be that way? Why is it that my presence does not matter to anyone?

All the people who were gathered there were busy in their own conversations, locked in their own small worlds, almost as if they couldn't see me, even after they had spoken to me.

I looked at my hands. My daughter was still there with me, holding on tightly, watching me with those wide, questioning eyes, wondering what I was up to.

I remember having walked a long way to be here. But now, it seems like the past.

It feels like I have arrived at a moment in my past, like I've stepped back into something I can't fully remember but can still feel. All of this matter and energy that surrounds me—it doesn't mean anything to me anymore. I should not be here.

*Where am I?* The question popped again, sharp and cold.

---

I thought about going back to the lady in the kitchen and asking her. Maybe she would tell me. But I knew I did not want that.

---

I wanted to get out of this place, but I did not move. My legs refused to listen, heavy and unresponsive, as if rooted to the floor. So, I stood there, trying hard to reach for something I could not get a hold of—something slipping through my fingers like water.

I stood there, lost, the confusion thick like fog around me, and in that unbearable pain of not knowing, I realised—no one would tell me where I am.

I stood there waiting for help. I stood there hoping someone—anyone—would just tell me who I am.

*Yes, please, who am I?*

As I stand here, lost and alone, I realise I'm waiting for help. For someone to save me from this unbearable pain of confusion.

I'm left standing here, waiting for something that probably may never come.

Did I say waiting?

What am I waiting for?

I can't really put my finger on that.

This short story **'Memory'** is very dear to my heart, no matter how many others I may write.

I deeply care for people who are struggling to hold on to their precious memories, sometimes small, sometimes the most important ones; forced to put on a smile even when you know, 'you don't know.'

This short story is dedicated to all of you, who suffer silently in holding together your memories in little and big ways.

Seek help if and when you need and extend a hand to those who may need it too.

The below website is only a guide to get some information.

dementia.org.au

Love,

# Rose Butterfly

# STORY #3

# A TWO LOVE STORY

Love happens unexpectedly!

## What I'm about to share might seem unusual and hard to believe.

If it were someone else's story, I might have thought the same. But when it's your own life and when things unfold in ways you never planned, you don't quite know what to make of it. You just hold on and accept that life sometimes leads you to places you could never have imagined.

People, relationships, beliefs—everything can take on a new form when it's *your* experience. It can quietly redirect your life into paths that feel unbelievable when you try to explain them to others.

---

And when all that dramatic, twisted story is yours, it doesn't feel like drama anymore. It feels like a tender, delicate narrative—a thread of life you carry close to your heart.

---

I live in a busy city, though what counts as *busy* probably depends on who you ask. Like any place, it has its good days and its bad days.

Sometimes the traffic feels like a living thing, loud and relentless. People get impatient, and the rains when they arrive, don't just fall, they pour like they own the streets.

But then there are quieter days, when everyone minds their own business, strangers are unexpectedly kind, and the day retires softly.

For me, I'm happy being here. Maybe it's because I've already made peace with the pace of life. Maybe it's because I've found my rhythm, a rhythm that works for me. Or perhaps, I'm just beginning to truly live for the first time.

---

I've built a routine I actually enjoy, and that alone gives me a sense of purpose. I wake up each morning looking forward to what's ahead.

---

My mornings start simply: making breakfast, brewing a cup of tea, and sending my husband off to work, often packing his lunch while I'm at it. It's such a small ritual, but it sets the tone for my entire day.

After that, I step into my own world. I run online exercise sessions for women, mostly homemakers wanting to shed a little weight and stay fit.

A handful are new mothers, women learning to trust their bodies again, eager to do what's right for them in this fragile stage after childbirth.

Fitness has been part of my life for over a decade now, though I never imagined it would become *my* life.

It started quietly, during my college years, when I joined a gym as a trainee. What was supposed to be just a side hustle slowly became something I cared about. Something I could see myself growing into.

---

Looking back now, it feels like one of those unexpected bends in the road—one you'd never plan, but that somehow delivers you to a place better than you imagined.

---

I met my husband at the gym, where I was working, and he was one of the regular visitors. What began as simple, casual conversations at the reception desk or near the treadmill slowly grew into deeper, more meaningful talks.

Before either of us even realised, we were spending more and more time together. Somewhere in between the laughter and easy conversations, we became close friends—comfortable, trusting, and genuinely happy in each other's company.

Within a year, we decided to get married. Not because we were head-over-heels in a wild, dramatic romance, but because it just felt right. It wasn't a whirlwind; it was a choice—steady and certain, a decision that felt more like stepping into a safe home than chasing an unpredictable spark.

And that choice turned out to be one of the best decisions of my life. When I married him, I knew him only as a good man, a decent, kind person. But living with him showed me so much more.

I learned how thoughtful, funny, and surprisingly warm-hearted he really was. Life with him wasn't just steady, it was joyful, often filled with little surprises that made the ordinary days feel special.

We could sit and talk for hours about anything: dreams, books, silly jokes, even the mundane things like what to cook for dinner and yet it all felt new and alive.

I often catch myself thinking how beautiful my life has become with him, richer and fuller than I could have ever imagined back when we first met.

One morning, just before leaving for work, he casually mentioned that one of his old college friends would be dropping by at our place in the evening. Then, with a cheeky grin, he added, *"You already know who I'm talking about, you've heard enough stories about him."*

I immediately knew who he meant. "The Casanova guy?" I asked, raising an eyebrow, half-joking but still surprised.

"Come on," he chuckled, "don't put it like that. He's a good guy and a good friend too."

"Fine," I said with a small laugh. "The friend who is more good than he is a Casanova."

He shook his head, still smiling at me, and said, "You could make or buy some snack for tea, but he might get here before I do." His face softened slightly, almost apologetic.

---

That meant I would have to receive this man I had never met—alone—and entertain him until my husband returned.

---

"Okay," I replied, carefully keeping any hint of irritation out of my voice. I didn't want to sound unwelcoming, but I also wasn't completely thrilled about greeting him at home on my own.

I had never met this man before, though I'd heard plenty about him. Stories of how carefree he was, how he lived unbound by anything or anyone.

A classic bachelor type, a charmer who never intended to settle down, happy living life without responsibilities.

I had heard about him many times from my husband, their crazy hangouts, the silly adventures, all the old "college boys" stories where this man often took centre stage. But despite all the stories, I had never been eager to meet him.

Honestly, guys like him don't interest me. Hopeless 'Romeos' who are all charm and sweet words until the thrill fades, never my kind of personality.

I don't find it exciting. I don't find it endearing. In fact, I find it a little pointless.

Did his stories ever fascinate me? No. There was nothing fascinating, interesting, or even remotely curious about him. Absolutely nothing.

You might think I'm exaggerating, but it's true, he never crossed my mind outside of those casual conversations.

Even when my husband told those old friendship tales, they didn't stick with me. He was just background noise in someone else's memory.

So, in my mind, he was a stranger, not just in my life, but also in my thoughts. A man who held no space in my memory or my heart.

"Dropping by," I repeated in my head.

'That's fine,' I told myself, 'I'll make something small for tea. Nothing fancy. Just something quick and easy, that should do.'

In the evening, I remembered about the whole *'dropping by'* plan, so I went straight to the kitchen and quickly put together something simple.

A handful of gram flour, some finely chopped spinach and onions—and just like that, I made a small batch of crispy bhajiya.

Not too much, just enough for the three of us— me, my husband, and the infamous friend I'd heard so much about.

I had barely finished arranging the last of the bhajiya on a plate when I heard the sound of a knock at the door.

"Already?" I muttered under my breath, slightly irritated.

I glanced at my clothes—they had spots of dough on them from the quick cooking.

*Great timing,* I thought, *couldn't he be five minutes late so I could at least change?*

Then I shook it off. *He's just a friend visiting. He's not going to analyse my dough-smeared clothes.* I made a quick reasoning in my head and went to open the door.

"Hello," he said, smiling pleasantly as I opened it.

---

I noticed his smile—genuine and warm, the kind you don't expect from someone you've only heard about through slightly judgmental stories.

---

*Looks are deceiving,* I reminded myself quickly.

"Come in," I said, stepping aside.

We sat down for tea and snacks, and to my surprise, the conversation flowed easily. He was humble, polite, and didn't have even a hint of arrogance about him.

This wasn't what I had imagined at all. He didn't come across as the sort of guy who would casually dump girls and move on like it was nothing.

He asked about my online fitness classes, listening with genuine curiosity.

"That's clever of you," he said, "to do it online and still have the rest of the day free for other things you enjoy."

It was flattering, and unexpected, to hear such words from him. I asked him what had brought him to our little city.

"Work and then… I guess work and also, I thought it would be great to catch up with an old friend," he said with an easy smile.

"That's true and nice. You're meeting him after a long time, I guess?" I asked.

"Yeah, it's been more than two years," he replied casually.

"What kind of work brought you here?" I asked.

He straightened slightly in his chair, a subtle spark of pride showing in his eyes.

"Too many hotels are rising up in this place," he explained. "My company has taken up the interior designing for a few big projects. I'm here to oversee things for a few days."

We talked a lot, about his work, about life in general and before I knew it, time had slipped past quietly.

I realised my husband still hadn't returned from work, but I wasn't uncomfortable at all. In fact, I was enjoying the conversation.

And I could tell, from the ease in his body language and the softness in his tone, that he was enjoying it too.

---

*Girl dumper!* I reminded myself. This is the guy who never sticks around. Don't fall for the polite act.

---

But it was difficult to align that thought with the person in front of me. He seemed so genuine, so kind, so... real.

It felt like there were two voices inside me. One, cautious and reminding me of everything I'd heard about him; the other, rebellious and dismissive, simply enjoying the moment.

'I don't care what you tell me,' that stubborn voice inside me said. If you want to think he's a "girl dumper," go ahead. But I will look only at what I feel right now—he's real, gentle, and there's a special kind of comfort in his presence.

"Bloody stubborn heart," I muttered quietly to myself.

I could feel how well we connected. It was strange, like we had known each other long ago, lost touch, and were now just picking up from where we left.

It was in that moment that my husband finally came home from work.

The two men lit up on seeing each other, laughter and quick hugs exchanged like no time had passed.

And because it was already late, my husband turned to his friend and said, "Stay for dinner."

---

"I haven't cooked dinner," I whispered to my husband when I got a chance, leaning slightly towards him so the words wouldn't carry.

---

"That's okay, we'll order from out," he whispered back with a quick reassuring smile.

So, we ordered in—*butter chicken and fried rice*. Yes, that odd little combination was something we had grown to love, our go-to comfort meal when cooking slipped off the day's agenda.

As we sat around the dining table, my husband turned to his friend and, in a teasing tone, said,

"Why, man, why are you still living amidst all that pollution and traffic? Stay here instead. You know there are enough and more opportunities here."

"Maybe his girlfriend is there," I added casually, smiling as I joined the banter.

"True," he replied, without missing a beat.

That one word—*true*—hit my heart in a strange, unexpected way.

When I had made that comment, it was just playful chatter, no thought behind it. But the moment I heard him say it, a tightness grew inside me, like a string being pulled a little too hard.

---

My face narrowed slightly, almost involuntarily. Did they notice? I don't know. Maybe they did but dismissed it as nothing.

---

"You decided to settle finally? I don't believe this," my husband said, looking surprised.

"I was just kidding, you know me," he replied with that gentle, disarming smile again.

After he left that evening, my husband turned to me, curious as ever, "So, what do you think of the so-called Casanova friend?"

He always said I was a good judge of character.

"He's alright," I said quickly, almost too quickly, and changed the topic before he could read my expression.

But over the days that followed, as he stayed in town for more than a week, he dropped by every day and I looked forward to it more than I would admit, even to myself.

We would sit on the sofa, conversations flowing so easily that hours would pass unnoticed.

We teased each other, laughed, and wandered into deeper talks—about life, spirituality, movies, cricket. There was *always* something to say to him, as though no topic was ever out of reach.

Sometimes, we stepped out together, escaping into a world that felt strangely our own, just for those brief moments.

Whenever he was around, I felt something stirring, a mix of deep intimacy and a fierce protective instinct I couldn't fully understand.

"I have never come across anyone by your name," he said one evening, his voice thoughtful, reflective.

"You mean, from the thousands and thousands of girls you've dated, not a single one?" I teased, smirking at him.

"Thousands would be an exaggeration," he said with a soft chuckle, "but yes, not met anyone by your name." He held my gaze as he said it, his eyes steady on mine.

And in that quiet exchange, I knew what we were experiencing was something beyond casual attraction.

It was an intimacy that felt raw and unexplainable, like love but on a level I couldn't yet define.

It should be wrong to feel this way.

Completely wrong.

I am committed to someone else—not just committed but married—to a man who is absolutely wonderful, who has done nothing but love and respect me.

So, it is wrong at *all* levels.

Still… still, I couldn't stop liking this person.

How do you stop liking someone?

Was there even a way to do that?

Then I thought—*was it really so wrong to enjoy someone's company?*

Was it his fault that he visited me every day?

Or was it my mistake that I encouraged him to come over and spend time with me?

I don't think either of us thought too much about it. *I think it is my fault.*

I welcome him every single day, smiling every time, unable to hide my love and respect for him.

---

Tomorrow, I told myself, I would put up a different face. I would make it clear that I had no feelings for him, that he was just my husband's friend and nothing more.

---

I made a solid promise to myself.

The next day, I waited eagerly—*too eagerly*.

I wanted to prove something, not to him, but to myself.

When he came, I greeted him differently, coldly even: "Hello, it's good to see you. Your friend will be late when he gets back."

He looked at me, a little confused.

"Are you alright?" he asked, his tone uncertain.

"What do you mean? I'm good. Last night we slept very late, and today we have some plans for the evening. I can't wait for him to get back," I said, forcing excitement into my voice.

"That's nice," he responded softly.

"What's the plan?" he asked, casually enough.

"Why?" I asked back, sharper than I intended.

"I was thinking if I could join you guys," he said.

"What?" I said aloud, startled.

---

I hadn't expected that. His words felt like something I wasn't prepared to deal with.

---

"Can I join you guys?" he repeated, slower this time, almost careful, as if making sure I heard him right.

"Why?" I asked again.

He looked at me with a slight tilt of his head, confusion flashing in his eyes. "Why?"

"I mean, why would *you* want to join?" I said, putting an odd emphasis on *you*.

"Ouch! That hurts. Don't you want me to join?" He smiled, but there was a vulnerability in it.

"Why would *I* want you to join?" I said, this time emphasizing *I*.

"I thought you would," he replied softly.

"I enjoy the alone time with my husband," I said firmly, holding my chin a little higher than usual.

"Alright, that's good. So… are you busy today?" he asked, still sounding friendly, still gentle.

For a moment, it seemed like he was going to leave, and my heart sank unexpectedly.

I didn't want him to leave.

"No, I'm not too busy," I replied quickly.

---

"You have plans for the evening and if you have things to do, I can carry on," he said, still as warm and open as before.

---

"It's okay, I don't have many things to do," I replied.

And that was the beginning of a new feeling— *pure joy* at not letting him leave, at having him stay by my side, spending yet another day with him.

I was *so glad* he didn't walk away.

We forgot about the awkward conversation and went back to our old rhythm—talking, laughing, losing track of time, forgetting the world outside that little bubble of ours.

Every evening when my husband got back, I would simply say, "Your friend dropped by," and he would smile and remark, "That's nice."

Then we would have dinner, retire for the night, and I would secretly look forward to the next morning.

To see him again.

To see *that* infamous friend.

Two weeks passed, and it was time for him to return.

---

I knew this day would come, but I wasn't sure how I would feel when it did.

---

To be honest, even in that moment, I wasn't sure what I was feeling.

The past few days had been wonderful. *Too* wonderful, spending time with him.

It had felt real, true, and strangely comforting.

But I didn't know what to make of it.

He said he was going back, and I wished him good luck.

He looked at me for a few seconds, and I acted cool, pretending like nothing inside me was trembling.

Before he was about to board the flight, he called me on my mobile from the airport.

My husband was sitting on the sofa in the living room, completely relaxed, reading a book.

I told my husband softly, "It's your friend."

He looked up briefly from his book and motioned with his hand to go ahead and take the call.

He didn't seem particularly interested in taking that call himself or, perhaps more accurately, it felt like he *wanted* me to be the one to answer it.

I sat down on the chair at the dining table and placed the phone to my ear.

"I'm at the airport… going to board the flight," he said, his voice carrying an odd hesitation. "But I'm thinking… if I should leave?"

"You should leave," I replied softly. "You have your job, your life. You're all settled there."

"Yes, I have my job… and heaps of work to complete. But I'm still thinking… if I should stay back," he said again, as though hoping I might give him a different answer this time.

"There might be people expecting you," I commented, trying to keep my voice even.

"Maybe…" he said quietly.

"See, that's a reason to go," I told him gently.

"There are also reasons to stay back," he countered, his voice even softer now.

---

"How many reasons do you have, to stay back?" I asked, trying to sound firm.

---

"One," he said, his voice low and full of something deeper. "Just one." He repeated it again, slower, like it meant everything.

"Is it a strong enough reason?" I enquired carefully.

"Too strong," he answered, almost in a whisper.

I could sense it—his heart, heavy and overflowing with love, with something unspoken yet powerful.

"I have an idea… How about you don't go?" I said.

"That makes more sense," he replied quickly. "Maybe I will stay back." He took a deep breath, as if a weight had lifted off him.

"For another week?" I asked, half hopeful, half afraid.

"No… like forever," he said, his tone calm and clear, like it was a decision already made.

---

I felt relieved on hearing that he had decided to stay back, the thought of seeing him again and spending time with him was something that I wondered would ever happen.

---

I was overjoyed.

But then I quickly realised the stupidity of my thoughts, the insensitivity of my heart. How could I ever encourage something like this.

What am I even doing?

Is this right or is it wrong?

I was feeling vulnerable and weak.

I hung up the call and glanced at my husband.

He was still calmly reading his book, unbothered, serene.

Without thinking too much, I walked towards him and stood beside him, almost seeking strength.

He lovingly held my hand and asked softly, "What happened?"

I hesitated, then said quietly, "He is not going back."

My husband smiled, looking at me with eyes so full of love. "Don't worry," he said gently.

---

"I understand. I am with you in everything you love and in everything you don't."

---

My eyes immediately filled with tears.

The weight of my emotions came crashing down and I wept like a child.

"What should I do? I'm sorry, I don't know what to do…" I said, broken.

"Be free," he said calmly. "I am with you. Don't be scared. I love you."

His voice was composed, his words warm, steadying me in ways I didn't even know I needed.

"I don't understand... I cannot understand your love," I cried softly into his shoulder. "It's more than I can imagine... more than I deserve."

He stroked my hair tenderly and whispered, "I love you... that's all I know. And I cannot deny anything that you love."

"Are you not mad at me?" I asked, my voice small, frightened.

"No," he said, and laughed—a light, unbothered laugh. "Not at all. I know you love me."

And in that moment, everything I felt for him magnified, multiplying a hundred times over.

I clung to his arms, the safest place in the world, my heart aching yet comforted.

He held me gently and said, "I tell you again... and if you want, I will tell you again and whenever you are doubtful, I will tell you again.

I am with you and will always love you, and all that you love."

I leaned closer, my lips near his ear, and whispered with a tearful smile, "You have a **bloody stubborn heart**."

*A Two Love Story* is a dedication to love without barriers. People who have broken norms to be with their love, people living as a throuple or in a triad, in unison, in understanding.

How is it possible?

The world doesn't know, they just wonder. But you have still got it all going, you got that special power installed in your heart. I am in wonderment of that kind of capacity to love and accept and defy all odds. I admire your strength.

Even when I cannot grasp, I will choose to be a soul in awe of your love, just like how I am in awe of the many wonderful things of this beautiful world.

Sincerely,

# Rose Butterfly

# STORY #4

# PEOPLE OF COLOURS

Click. Post.

## She wore a stunning red lipstick; the dark Kajal lined inside those roundly shaped eyes made it more vivid that they were big and beautiful.

To top it, her eyelashes were curled. Her brows were tinted brown and were in perfect shape.

Her cheeks were painted slightly pink, and she added a special shine onto it that made it look healthy.

She let her hair down, it was silky, thick, and black.

And then like every other day, she gave that smile, with that mesmerizing look in her eyes, her lips held so perfect in position and then she clicked.

**The selfie.**

---

I wanted to speak to her and tell her that I watched her every day.

---

I wanted to tell my friend my thoughts.

My dear, you may observe the lives of other people who in certain moments may seem to mirror your own.

They may reflect your emotions, express feelings that resonate with you, speak and sigh in ways that you feel familiar.

You'll see them sharing stories, laughing, connecting in ways that stir something deep within.

But amidst it all, there's one question you must ask yourself.

Where are you?

Is your story the same as theirs, or do you have a unique identity?

______________________________________

Does the likeness that you share with other people all around the world hold you back from experiencing who you truly are?

______________________________________

The world consists of people.

People of all colours.

Colours representing their life moments, phases, stages and emotions. And these colours further have shades, and the shades have tones, and you may have passed through many of it.

Now or at some point in your life.

The person you see in front of you is both unlike you and yet so much like you. This is the paradox and the normality of the world.

People peeking into each other's lives, sometimes with purpose, other times without meaning.

At one point someone may come closer, and you may feel connected and then one day all of it disappears.

These invisible threads connect and repel us, and we are all a prey to it.

And somehow, all of this feels perfectly normal. The world continues on, each interaction fitting seamlessly into the fabric of existence, as though this chaotic blend of closeness and separation is the only way it could ever be.

Everything around you seems sane, grounded in the rhythm of everyday life.

Yet, lurking beneath this veneer of normalcy is a subtle madness—the insanity that thrives within the confines of what we call 'sane'.

The true absurdity lies not in the chaos but in how effortlessly we accept it as ordinary.

Let me ask you again, in the middle of this chaos, where are you?

You don't know?

You should know. It is important for you.

I am talking to you.

Why are you acting like you can't hear me?

Are you afraid?

Of whom?

The world. I see.

And the world is...

Isn't it in your pocket? Then why are you so afraid? I laughed.

She did not understand my joke.

You need to take care of your soul.

Are you listening to me my friend?

I see her.

Once again, even when she ignores my presence.

The selfie is the routine of her most mornings. She knows how to give that perfect look; she has done it like a hundred times.

Does that selfie hide anything? The one that she shares with the world, to feel connected. Does it hide anything?

**Who will ever know, except her.**

---

Let us look at her more broadly without her permission, from an angle that she does not want us to see.

---

Maybe we can gauge her with the shallowness that she sees herself.

The selfie clearly showed her face, the sensuality of her eyes, full lips, and the beautiful hair.

What it did not show was an inch of her plump figure, her untoned arms, her flabby stomach, and her short stature.

**How ugly! Isn't it?**

Would a wider shot take a perfect picture?

---

No, I guess. But for now, only she knows it. And us. Because we decided to look into that picture from a different viewpoint.

---

Her face steals the thunder.

But her spirit can take it away. She tries hard, but her selfie fades into the background, out of sight and out of mind.

She looked at the clicked pictures. They aren't that perfect.

'Did I not give the right angle?

Did I not hold in the right muscle, where did that click go wrong?' She thought to herself, then murmured something to herself.

She clicked once again.

"Got it right, this time?" I jumped in with my question.

"Shut up", she shouted.

Then she sat with that picture for a while and then posted it with a good morning message in her groups and got ready to go to the bank.

---

"Why didn't you use any filter today?" I interfered again. Obviously, I had my doubts.

---

"There's so much light from the window. Its great!" She clarified.

**Ah, stupid me! I thought. There is so much for me to learn when it comes to taking a picture.**

"Why do you take pictures only in one angle?" I asked her.

"The other one makes me look fat." She said sadly.

"But you are fat." I said and laughed.

I thought that it was funny she felt that the angle made her look fat.

I couldn't stop laughing at it, so I literally rolled over and laughed.

---

"I hate you. I hate you. Get out of here!" She shouted.

---

"Chubby lady, short lady

fat, and round.

Look at your curves,

look at your hooves.

Look at your moves

Every time you move around" I sang with my heart out.

"What a disgusting song you made out of me?" She yelled like she was in pain.

Aghast! I am shocked. Why don't you like this song? I asked her. But she looked so upset like I was being mean to her.

"You are afraid of mean words from people around. Is that your problem? Is that your problem my friend?" I once again confronted her.

But that was not well received. She got back at me, screaming, "You mock me."

"I disapprove. You mock yourself." I retorted.

---

But she wasn't ready to hear anything that I spoke. She wasn't even ready to hear out herself.

---

She left the room, the house.

Left behind a soul, a spark that was waiting to light.

At the customer service desk, she is a middle-aged woman, attending calls, unnoticed by the people around her, despite her large locks of hair, big eyes and that strong red lipstick.

She tries to fit in, with an awkward smile on her face but somehow, she is invisible.

Nothing makes her stand out because there is so much of imperfection in her. There is nothing charming about her.

That selfie is not entirely her; it shows only that bit of something or the only thing that is attractive about her, and that's all she's got.

A selfie face clicked with a lot of lighting.

But her unproportioned figure is ugly and that's what the world sees and that's what makes her unnoticeable.

---

She glanced at her phone several times, watching the usual stream of comments and likes roll in.

---

But none of it was enough to keep a lasting smile on her face because what she truly longed for, felt out of reach—something she never believed she could find.

Her face looked gloomy like she was always in some sad thoughts. Trying to reach someone, longing for something.

Who would look at her, amidst all the flawless women around, and then turn to her and say the words she so desperately longs to hear?

You are beautiful inside and out.

You are the most important person in my life.

You are my world! I love you so much.

Who would ever say those words to her?

How could she ever find someone who could make her feel truly seen and cherished in that way?

She continued her work in silence.

Her lipstick had faded, the kajal smudged slightly beneath her tired eyes. Her hair had lost its morning shine, and her posture had slouched under the weight of the day.

It was evening, she yawned feeling exhausted.

---

Tiredly she checked her phone once more, hoping for something, anything. But after a while, the screen had remained still—silent.

---

My dear friend, how I wish you could hear me. Then, I would tell you to accept that burning soul that lies within you and to see yourself for the wonder that you are.

Cherish that magnificence that only you hold and enjoy who you are.

Be ruled not by the world but by love.

My fat friend, I love you.

**When** you look for that perfect click, to find that perfect picture to post, what you leave behind is a spirit that is bubbling to experience you in your true self.

I consider **People of colours** the most repulsive of all my short stories. But let me stop there and understand that I am still one among many.

This short story is a call, to wake up and connect with yourself. Embrace that spirit and chuck the false click. Laugh aloud and cherish the time. Perfection lies in every uncompromised moment.

Ugly is never anybody. Ugly can only be an attitude or an action.

Rest everything is only beauty, beauty & beauty.

Unfiltered,

# Rose Butterfly

# STORY #5
# THE COOK

Behind all that silence, there's a strong-willed lady

**I walked briskly into the kitchen; it was tiny and a narrow little space. It was also dark and maybe a little unkept.**

It had an air of neglect, with pans hung randomly on the walls, a small cutting slab to work on and a medium sized wash basin. On the shelves, there were many serving dishes but only a few vessels for me to cook the food.

The walls had a particular blend of green and blue, and the floor was wooden and sometimes a bit creaky.

It wasn't a well-ventilated space, so it seemed like there was always something burning.

---

One looks at this kitchen, and one may not feel like stepping in or working here. But for me, I am used to this place now.

---

I do remember walking in here and being totally uncomfortable about everything around me, but now I am alright.

I go along with it because I am used to it, and also I am not sure what else to do.

I put down my things and looked around, thinking about what to make for the day. The kitchen is where I spend most of my time. It is where I feel I can do something magical. Even though it is a solitary space, I am connected to every little thing here.

In this tiny room, I am alone amidst the dishes, food, spices and tools.

I am like a ghost in the attic. Nobody really sees me or speaks to me.

But they know I am here. They acknowledge me, they say their orders and that's it. That is all is required.

A strong smell always lingered in the air. I can't tell if it was the place itself or a mix of the room's essence and my own presence.

But all of this is okay. Despite everything that may seem not okay, I still love it.

Because when I am here, what matters is my work. The smell, the dampness, the mess, all of that is kept aside to do what is important-- my job, my skill, what makes me who I am.

Here, I am the Cook.

The person in charge to put a smile on every customer that walks out of this place.

Even when I am stuck here for endless hours, I cannot stop being the craftsman, the artist. I have to do the best every single time because when it comes to food, it is described as divine and heavenly. So absolutely no place for mistakes.

I put on my Apron and was ready for the day.

That is me, ready and on time every day without any complaints.

From morning till night, it is busy here. For a small restaurant, I would say it is doing quite well. I do not know all of the aspects of how a restaurant works. But from my perspective, it is always a busy day.

I come here and I cook like an artist at work, or a dancer who dances for her audience. Every day I peek through my window to get a glance of the people walking into the restaurant. They are my audience to whom I have to perform. I have to make them happy.

So, I watch them for a while. All kinds of people walk into the restaurant—sad, happy, cheerful, thoughtful. Some walk in eagerly to share some exciting news, while others clearly aren't in the mood for conversation.

Some are too hungry and frustrated, and they just want the food. Others seem to be here simply to pass time, as if they are hiding from something.

They all can get very loud at times, some talking to each other, some on the phone and then there are the quiet eaters.

But at some point, in the middle of all of this madness, there comes a moment, a quiet moment.

I call it the 'divine break.'

It is a time when all the customers are in sync, fully immersed into the act of enjoying the food, mesmerised by the taste of it. They get completely lost in the moment, forgetting who they are with and where they are. In this moment they are just enjoying the food, satisfying their hunger, and soaring in pleasure.

Sometimes, I don't see any of this, the people or the divine break. I am too caught up in my work that I don't get a chance to get a glimpse of the drama. However, later I think about it. I think 'I should have looked at who walked in; I should know my audience.' When I serve, I need to know at least a few faces to imagine how they would enjoy the food. The faces are an inspiration while I cook.

I miss the chance to look at them only because of how too tied up I get in the kitchen not just cooking but later clearing it as well.

---

I like it when I can imagine their faces happy and satisfied with a meal. For me I believe that what I serve is not just food but something that is like a hug to their soul.

---

Throughout the day, I am on my foot, my hair up, my T-shirt a bit sweaty and my eyes bloodshot from the hot air of the kitchen.

Still, I never skip to admire something, a little secret that only I enjoy. All the while I work, I glance and admire the beauty of my golden bracelet dancing on my right-hand while I stir my dishes.

What's so special about my bracelet?

When I see my hands adorned with that bracelet, I feel a deep connection to myself. It's more than just jewelry—it feels like an extension of me, a source of power that helps me glimpse the bigger picture of who I truly am. It reminds me that I have a beautiful face, even though it's currently shrouded in the darkness and discomfort of this place.

I also feel it is this magical string that makes all dishes extra special.

My slender body manages to move through all of what is required for the day without any rest.

There are big pots on the stove and stacked up raw materials which I will arrange while I am cooking.

There are also things spread on the floor which I will have to clear later, but first task would be to plan the meals for the day.

---

I am responsible for everything that goes out from the kitchen to the customers. Whatever I serve, I do it with love, and I try to do it to my best.

---

At the end of the day, I get so tired that I leave few things for the morning. Hence all the piled-up mess and the things on the floor.

As a cook, I love every person that walks into the restaurant.

Sorry not everyone.

Not everyone.

There is one person whom I do not like. Actually, I dislike him.

**THE VISITOR**

Every now and then, I get a visitor in the kitchen—not just any visitor, but the owner of the restaurant himself. His presence is impossible to miss. He doesn't just walk in quietly; he makes an entrance with a loud voice and a laugh that is unfriendly.

---

When he arrives, it's to inspect what
I've been cooking and to dictate what
I should and shouldn't be doing.

---

He's a hefty man with a noticeable belly, and a commanding tone.

Every time he speaks to me, there is not an ounce of respect, nor any regard for the long hours I spend standing on my feet, working in this cramped kitchen. It is as if all it means nothing and it is expected that I work that way.

He comes there to command. To show that I am dispensable and a mere worker who is at the mercy of the boss.

What I had served yesterday was much liked by the people, I could hear them talking about it.

Sometimes I can hear them shouting out.

**"Today's was simply fabulous!"**

That compliment is meant for me.

They want me to hear, so they shout it out.

So, I shout back.

"Thanks!"

---

On days when customers lavish praise on the food, you can almost guarantee 'the visitor' will show up the next day.

---

One might think it is to compliment me. But that's not the case with this visitor. He comes like a spy, to check on what magic I am creating and how?

He knows people have praised my cooking, and he visits to make sure all of it doesn't go to my head. He glances around the kitchen as if he is searching for something.

Maybe he thinks I'm hiding a genie that does the work for me.

Or does he think I have a secret ingredient? Whatever it is, only he knows what he is up to.

This morning, I'd completely forgotten about last night's compliments and the buzz around the dishes. I came in like I do every day—to cook, to serve, and to get through the shift.

After a while, the visitor walked in, his white shirt unbuttoned down to his chest, revealing his thick dark chest hair.

His big moustache and vulture-like eyes gave an awkward presence.



I quickly realized why he'd come—word of last night's praise must have reached him. He would have wanted to make sure how things are at work today.

He came in and asked, "So what is it today?"

I showed him the neatly cut fish, marinated with garlic, chillies, and spices, the vegetables cut for salad, the bread, the meat soup, and the baked potatoes that would go very well with the rest.

It smelled good and I knew it would taste even better. I had no doubts. The visitor looked restless, like he did not know what exactly to tell me.

He lifted the lid off the dishes, eyeing it with a doubtful expression, as if to say it was merely adequate, nothing special.

Then, he took a spoon and poured a bit of the meat soup into his palms and licked it.

Finishing whatever was on his palms, he said "it's okay, alright, but you must try to make better food."

'Disgusting man! You show no respect to me or my food.' My head was on fire.

**But I chose to keep quiet.**

---

He had said something similar the last time too, I had heard it so many times now, so it shouldn't matter. But I was burning inside.

---

He continued, "I get a feeling that you do not have enough work here and you are getting lazier."

Look at this man, standing right in front of me. After squeezing himself into this tiny space where he can barely stand for a few minutes, he comes only to say these mean words, every single time he shows up.

The same man, the same talk, the same journey.

I took a deep breath. A cool sensation enveloped me. What happened next was instantaneous, no...not in anger, but in absolute peace.

An overwhelming feeling of happiness, realisation, and courage covered me up.

It pushed me. It moved me to a place where I felt strong enough to do the right thing.

---

I removed my Apron, hung it in its hook, looked at him, like as if for the first time, I was ready to see him and the ugliness he held. And then, I walked away.

---

"Hey, what are you doing?" I heard him say.

I continued to walk, smiling to the other people who worked there and also waving at the customers with a big smile.

I could hear the man say something. It was not clear or perhaps I did not pay enough attention.

I was not bothered or concerned.

I kept walking, I had no idea where I was heading to or what was I going to do next.

I was walking away from something that was my everyday routine. I was walking away from my comfort space, my work, my money, my identity.

I was walking away without any plan, or direction.

But at that point, I kept walking.

---

Because someone deep inside me, gently told me to.

---

And I chose to listen and obey.

Because that's what you do. Sometimes you obey others.

Sometimes you obey yourself.

**'The Cook'** is a story for you— The ones who are silent and working in unhealthy conditions because you have no choice. The ones who forgot to dream, the ones who are scared to walk away.

For those who found the courage to leave behind people, jobs, circumstances, and places. the ones who have left and feel left out.

What does it really mean to walk away? It's like a blank space in front of you with absolutely no clue.

Some may call it a blank canvas, ready for a new life, but the reality is it's a difficult and uncertain journey when you choose to change course.

My heart goes out for the strugglers, the path finders, the dreamers, the loners.

I am with you on this journey.

Truly,

# Rose Butterfly

# STORY #6
# THE GOLDEN DIVA

# Special Edition

**Over the years, I have met many celebrities, and I have taken many interviews. But this one was different.**

It was not like the usual meetings where I would be with the person, take the interview and get the hell out of there. Not that I did not enjoy what I did, just that sometimes the whole experience can be very empty.

I love meeting people, and I like to learn about them; besides the fact that it is also my job.

But right now, I am headed somewhere to meet someone very special and have a small chat, an exclusive piece just for me.

When I say just for me, it is truly only for me. To meet, listen and speak and never publish.

A onetime exclusive, only for me.

I was thrilled and at the same time a bit anxious. No one had accompanied me for the interview, because that was the deal that my friend had arranged.

A time with the very famous singer, artist, dancer- Golden Diva.

A time to spend with her, no paper and pen and absolutely no recording.

In a way it was strange because I was not going in as a journalist but just as myself and that could be challenging, not being a journalist beside a star like her.

My head was filled with thoughts and excitement was bubbling in my stomach. I loved it. I had not really done an interview solely for myself.

But where I am heading to now, was just for myself.

---

It was more of a secretive one and it had a unique feel, a kind of quietness in my heart. Like I do not have to worry about what to ask, I am under no pressure here.

---

This was all arranged by my very close friend from the music industry. I think he is too kind to do this for me.

But I know he did it for friendships sake, for love's sake and for music's sake. He did it because he knew I needed this.

I remember being in his office a few months back, with my head down on his desk and with a clouded mind.

Then him telling me, "Do an interview for your soul, meet someone you want to meet, do it for yourself and let no one know."

I looked up at him and asked shamelessly, "Do you think I can get an interview with Golden Diva like that?"

"Golden Diva Huh? You have very high expectations from me." He said with a doubtful face.

But I knew.  That doubtful face would still get it done.

So why am I meeting her?

---

She had agreed to meet me, allowing a little time for a curious admirer who wanted to know about her.

---

This meant, I could ask all that I wanted but never publish it out as an interview.

I was in for it.

I wanted to know who she was.

I had seen her only in pictures and she looked so mystique.

She never gives many interviews or goes for any talk shows.

Every time I see her on screen, I sense a kind of magic that she holds.

I was intrigued by it, and I wanted to know the story behind that magic. I wanted to know the secret of that captivating energy.

I had carefully organised what I had intended to ask her. Now all I need was to be there.

And here I was.

I was warmly greeted into her large mansion by a gentleman. He said his name was Tim and he was the manager.

> The house was too big and lavish with mirrors and high ceiling, chandeliers and artifacts. My eyes went into every corner of that house, and I could imagine her come out through somewhere.

I did not know when she would come or where she would come from and that made me feel a bit squeezy in the stomach.

I decided to sit and may be search through my bag to keep me busy and less anxious.

"Hello"

That was golden Diva.

I jumped up from my seat, looking blankly at her and really not understanding who she was.

She wore a white t-shirt, a grey cardigan, and a light blue Denim shorts. Her hair neatly tied up.

She looked thinner and very plain, nothing like I had imagined. But her face still lit an aura.

"Hi, I am Anna."

"Nice to meet you Anna, how has your day been?", She sounded casual.

---

She was so friendly, warm and sincere that I did not want to pretend either, so I said, "I was preparing myself to be here and meeting you. That's all my day has been about."

---

She looked at me with a gentle smile and spoke. "Come I will take you upstairs and we can chat there."

She asked Tim to arrange for some snacks and drinks, and we went upstairs.

We sat comfortably in a large visitor's room upstairs. It was cozy and had a large collection of books, music records, fresh flowers and some paintings on the wall.

As we sat down, our snacks arrived too. There was also orange juice, tea and coffee for us.

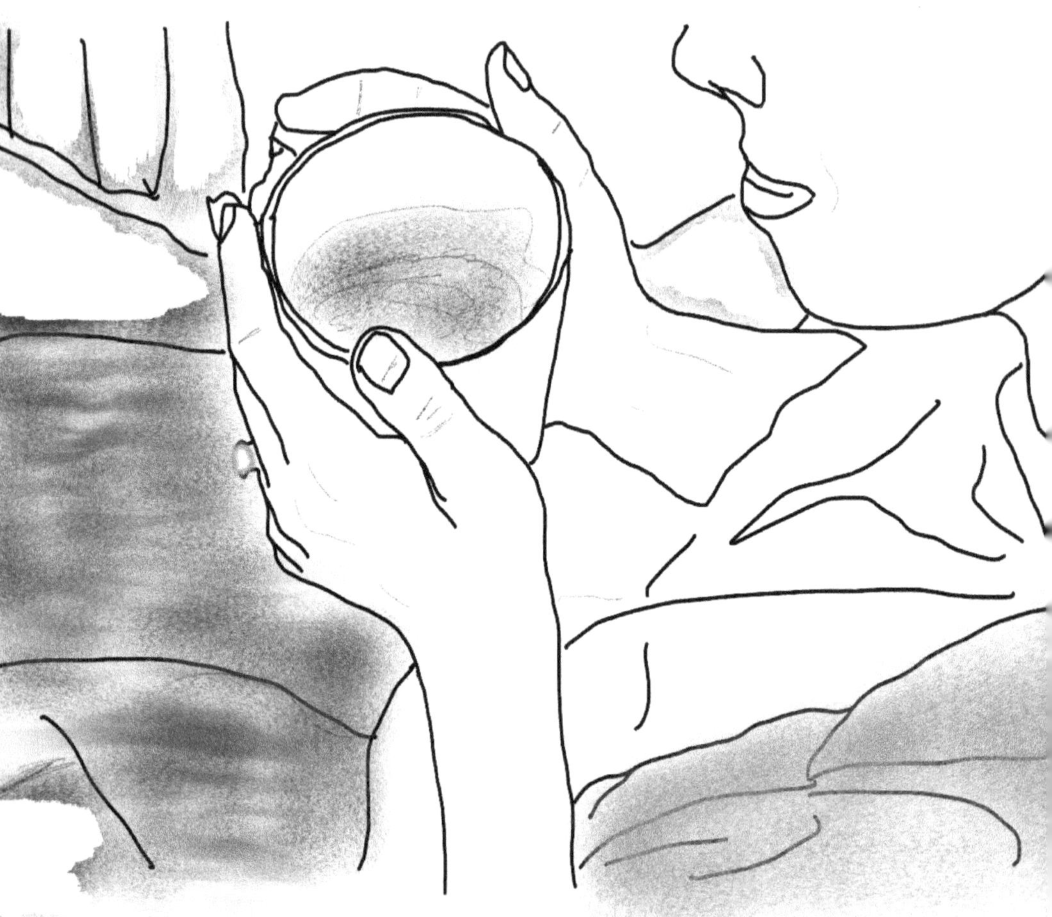

She had a cup of coffee, and I joined her. We both took a tiny quiche, and she asked a few things about me.

I was happy to tell her about me and wondered if it mattered to her.

But she listened to it all attentively asking me relevant questions. She is a good interviewer, I thought.

---

We moved from there and she quickly showed me her bedroom, her dressing room, her music room, a relaxation room, a room filled with paintings, and they all looked magnificent.

---

"Anna, you do know that you cannot give away the interview to anyone." She said politely.

"Yes, I know." I assured her.

"Good…. good. so then why?" She asked me with hint of curiosity in her eyes.

"It is still a big deal. You would understand if you were in my shoes." I said.

She laughed loud on hearing what I spoke and then she said, "All right, were you shocked to see me dressed very different?"

"Yes. I thought you would come in a golden dress or something." I told her.

"No, I don't wear golden dresses unless I don't want to be seen." She replied quickly

"But aren't you more glamorous in your golden dress, more visible?" I asked her.

In a very easy manner she said, "No, I am less visible."

I kept quiet for a moment, then asked.

"Tell me about your childhood."

---

She began to speak in a calm tone, "You know Anna, my parents died when I was around 16, I moved houses a lot. Nobody really wanted to take care of me.

---

I was like an extra piece in the houses where I stayed, and nobody knew where to put me.

I would wait for hours to be given a space to keep my things.

I would just stand not knowing what is expected from me.

I would keep thinking 'what am I to do? I wish somebody would guide me.'

No care, no attention, appreciation, nobody looked at me. Everybody was busy, probably they were.

I was alone in a big world full of people but not a single person to look at me and ask me how I was doing.

I have worked in a lot of places, then I began to sing in parties and bars, which eventually helped me. But that journey was not easy either.

I may not recollect much of it now, because I don't like to revisit those days.

But let me show you something."

---

She showed a burnt mark near her breasts, one dark one on her hand, two on her inner thighs.

---

"These were made by some of the men I went out with." She said in a sad reflective way.

I was shocked seeing them.

"Give me a minute Anna." Saying this she went into her dressing room.

I waited outside the room, a bit taken aback by what she shared. Then I saw her step out of her room.

She had changed her clothes; she had changed into a beautiful golden dress.

"How's the dress?" She asked with a smile.

"You look lovely. I have seen you with something similar in a picture, but I think you look so much more prettier in it in person." I said.

She continued like she never stepped a moment away, "They are gorgeous, aren't they?

Not many know, but I was married once.

I remember walking down the aisle, looking all very pretty and so very young. I was twenty. Too young!

I thought my world was made. Sometimes you never know what your world is until you move forward.

---

My husband, his name was Mark, used to cheat on me. I knew there was something that was not alright, but I always pushed it aside.

---

That feeling of gloom, sadness, something is not right always lingered with us.

One must listen to what your heart says.

Failed marriages can be exhausting. But again, that is an old tale, buried somewhere, and hurts at times."

She brushed her hair and tied it up, few strands left untied. She then beaded it with stones.

"Did you learn music?" I asked.

---

"I did as a child, that was when my parents were around. My parents were very sweet. Took care of me well.

---

My father said, he would always be there for me.

He was like a pillar of strength.

But not every time you can keep your promises, isn't it?

He died unable to keep his promise. Death can betray anyone."

"Yes," I said quietly.

She looked at me again and then motioned me to follow her.

It felt like she peeked into my heart, but she was kind enough to not ask me anything.

A very sensitive interviewer.

She put on her make up, her red blush, the dark liners on her eyes, red lipstick and colours spread on her face.

It looked like she was painting, an extraordinarily beautiful one.

My voice nearly broke when I asked her, "what happened to your mother?"

She looked at me, may be into my heart too, took a deep breath, closed her eyes, and turned away and spoke.

"My mother was heavily depressed after my father passed away; she was not able to manage anything. She just did not know how to handle the situation.

I began to hate her so much.

---

I remember I would plead her to cook, to wake up in the morning, come to my school on important days. But she would never do any of it.

---

I thought if she died I could do better in life. I think she sensed that. One day, she killed herself.

I don't know whether she did that because she loved me or she just didn't care about me. I would not know that.

I would like to believe it is love, but maybe it was fear, shame, guilt, lack of courage and no regard for me.

After mother died, I was mostly alone like I said moving from house to house.

------

I did not trust anyone, but I always chose to live. Because the journey is not over."

------

She put on a giant hat, it was golden and black, studded with stones. It covered a larger part of her face.

She then put on her gloves, made of velvet and a bracelet on top of the gloves on her right hand, a tiny one. Almost invisible around her large attire.

I could stare at her like that for hours but that would be awkward, so I asked her, "did you ever think of another career?"

"When I was young, I wanted to be a teacher. A science teacher and a scientist. But I could not study further because of how things went about.

In fact, I haven't even completed my schooling because of all that was going on with my mother. I had to move from one job after another to keep things moving and to survive.

Now I am living a dream come true life, but this is a dream that I never dreamt.

"What is your dream then?" I asked curiously

---

She closed her eyes and stood for a while; I could see her how happy she looked. I guess she was seeing her dream.

---

Then she opened her eyes, looked at me and said, "It's too beautiful to share. Will keep it safe with myself..."

I smiled at her, acknowledging that it's all hers. She smiled too and walked away to pick her shoes. It matched her dress. Golden and smooth.

As she wore them, she looked at me and said, "These shoes are made of chocolate, did you know?"

"Really?" I asked and looked closely at them.

"Nah, I am just kidding. If they were, they wouldn't be here," she said, giggling.

"I got to go for a meeting Anna; it was nice to be with you. But I got to go now." She said in an apologizing tone.

"Thank you so much for giving me your time and sharing so much." I tried to express my gratitude.

"Did you enjoy the snacks?" She enquired.

"Yes, but not as much as talking with you." I replied.

---

She laughed again and remarked; "you are a smart young lady. Let's go downstairs. I have meetings set for the rest of the day."

---

We went down and she waved goodbye to me and moved towards other people who were waiting for her.

I wandered around the room to see her again before I left.

She was not the woman I saw when I had come in, now she was the Golden Diva.

When she met me, she gave me the privilege to see her true self and her transformation.

Was she waiting to meet me like how I was waiting to see her? I thought.

Now she is the Golden Diva for everyone. Extravagant in style, larger than anyone in the room, taller than life.

Her face was not very visible because of her giant hat. But I could clearly see the red lipstick. I had seen her put on that.

I had seen her put on every bit of what she was that evening. In a moment it was all confusing. It was like I never met her, talked with her and she never shared anything.

Was that all real?

Or was it all a joke like the one she said about her shoes being made up of chocolate. Was she just kidding with me throughout?

No…Never. I remember, I saw her scars.

I pulled up my sleeves and looked at my hand. The scar from the accident was still very visible on my hand.

Nothing can hide that mark than a long sleeve. And to hide my tears I need a warm smile.

Death can betray anyone; I thought what the Diva had said.

___

I lifted my head from my thoughts and looked into the crowd again. I watched her talking, smiling and greeting people.

___

In this short time, I had gotten to know the diva a little and that was just great.

She caught me looking at her.

But as I looked at that face, I wasn't sure what that face held.

**Was it a smile? A smirk? A sorrow? Serenity? Victory?**

Or the yearning to chase a dream that is yet to be fulfilled! I will never know.

It is deeper, deeper inside somewhere.

Whatever that face held, the **Diva** had hid her **scars** well.

All my stories are dedicated to someone special. This one is for you! **The Golden Diva!**

The people who wake up every day despite knowing how hard it is going to be, taking up challenges, falling in defeat and still choosing to value the gift of life.

This story is for you, who are out in the world, hiding those scars of hurt, shame, suffering, lost, betrayal, and are putting on a smile, dealing with life and conquering everyday like a Diva.

Each one of you is a Golden Diva!

Love you all!

# Rose Butterfly

# STORY #7
# CRUSH

Are you willing?

## On a Saturday morning, after breakfast, the four of us began getting ready to head out.

'Getting ready' can become its own little storm sometimes. Everyone rushing in their own directions, trying to figure out what to wear, someone inevitably heading to the toilet at the very last minute, another person clearing the room because it somehow always needs clearing *right now*.

Meanwhile, I'm packing a few essentials, and amidst it all, the children are bursting with questions before they've even started getting ready themselves:

"Where are we going?"

"When will we be back?"

"Can we get something while we're out?"

Every single time, I have to remind them gently that until we actually step out of the house, everything is *just a plan*. The first step, I tell them, is to simply *get ready*.

I have a wonderful family.

My husband is a loving man. He cares about every part of me, about the tiniest aspects of my day-to-day life. This might sound like an exaggeration, but it isn't. He genuinely worries when he notices even the slightest crease of worry on my face. He loves to see me smile, and when I don't, he instantly picks up on it, like an emotional radar tuned only to me.

He is kind to a fault, always checking if I need help, always polite in his words, gentle in his tone.

Yes... he could easily be called a dream man.

I have two girls—one 12, the other 8. I wouldn't call them a handful, because they really aren't. They're pretty much on their own, curious explorers of life, figuring things out at their own pace—whether it's art, coding, or whatever currently fascinates them. Most days, they're learning through YouTube videos, soaking in everything, and then, in their sweet innocence, turning into my tiny life coaches, giving *me* advice about living!

When I pause and reflect on my life, I see someone who has everything in abundance. Truly everything, at least everything that most people would long for.

But there's one thing… something deeply personal. A feeling stuck within me, almost like an echo I hadn't noticed until recently.

I have a solid *male ego*.

---

It's strange to even say that out loud. One might never suspect it when they look at me, or even after knowing me for years. It isn't something you can detect at first glance or even second or third. It isn't obvious like a bad habit or a loud personality trait.

---

For me, it wasn't even identifiable from a young age. It's something that sneaks up on you, slowly.

It's a realisation that comes only when you begin to truly *look inward*—when you explore your own thoughts, watch your reactions, observe the little flashes of emotion that rise inside you and ask yourself *why*.

For a long time, I didn't recognise it in myself. Many of you might not either. You might have it but not know it yet.

It's only when life throws you into situations that poke at your quiet corners that you really see yourself—see what lies buried deep within, what leaps to the surface, and how all of it plays out in your head, then your heart, and then, unavoidably, on your face. And, eventually, if left unchecked, even on your health.

Is it bad?

No, not when everything is working in its favour and it is taken care of well.

> When that ego is nourished, you feel just fine, and if it was always nourished, you wouldn't even know you had one—until you hit a strong emotion.

But when all of that nourishment and support is not happening, the male ego suffers and crushes you into pieces.

You feel like you don't exist.

You feel helpless, less valuable.

You think you are not making enough contributions, your life feels meaningless, you feel invisible… and sometimes, in those low moments, you might even be tempted to end your life.

All because your male ego is suffering.

You are in pain, and you don't know how to deal
with this.

Can a woman have such a strong male ego?

While it's often more commonly associated with men, many women can exhibit traits typically attributed to a so-called male ego.

This might shape the way they think, what they desire, and how they perceive society.

---

Women with such an ego may not necessarily exhibit assertiveness but will often prioritise independence and control in a way that differs from traditional gender expectations—like me.

---

This tendency can lead them to think and behave differently from their female peers, challenging societal norms and conventional roles.

Their outlook may be more driven by power, achievement, and self-determination—traits often culturally linked to masculinity, but which are not inherently male.

This dynamic highlights that ego isn't gender-specific. Rather, it's a reflection of personal values, upbringing, and individual personality—something that transcends traditional gender stereotypes.

It also tells us about that diversity in thought and behaviour exists within both men and women.

Now, about me.

I am a woman who makes no financial contribution to the house.

The term *housewife* is rarely used these days, often replaced by *homemaker*.

Regardless of the label, I don't feel comfortable being defined by either.

When someone asks me *what I do*?

I see it as a painful question.

---

Also, not bringing in money to the household is disturbing for me—it creates a feeling of weakness and unpleasantness.

---

It is not like we need any additional money to run the house, but I think about it, and I feel hurt.

Something inside me gets hurt.

I think it's my ego.

My question often to myself is: *what is my worth if I am not bringing any money to my home?*

One may think that it is not right to assess one's own value based on financial contribution,

but what if you bring absolutely no money and have no wealth of your own?

Then who are you?

When you are not identified by the work you do, what is it about you that is so precious?

Is it simply that you are a life? A living being?

---

I know that children have no problem recognising their true worth—and it's absolutely beautiful how, without a doubt, they can demand anything, with an understanding that the entire world is theirs, that all its wealth belongs to them.

---

Sadly, I cannot think that way.

There is a small me with a big ego.

And that ego is like a thorn that crushes me now and then.

Sometimes by people, sometimes at occasions, at discussions, or by me... by my own thoughts.

My husband says, *"You have no idea how much you contribute to this family. You basically run this house. You take care of everyone."*

My kids think that I am too cool and would not trade for anything more than to be with me.

But what do I want?

Nothing much.

I just want to know my worth.

*How much would you pay me?*

*Who wants to hire me?*

*What do you think I am good at?*

It is not like I have not tried to get a job or have not tried to explore my skills,

but nothing works out for me, and my heart sinks down at every attempt and every fall...

and all of my efforts feel worthless.

Most times, I am okay because I bury my feelings and carry on with the day.

I think about my awesome family, and I feel I should let go of any bad thoughts that keep me away from enjoying my beautiful life.

But sometimes, my ego takes over.

Then I am a different person.

I go silent, sad, and depressed.

It affects me most when I step out, and I become aware of my incapacity.

I feel that everything I am buying is from the hard-earned money of my husband.

---

That thought is instilled in my core,
and that's what my heart beats:

---

*"You don't bring in any money, you are worthless."*

So here is me stepping out with my family today, in a black top and light blue jeans.

I wore a golden earring and left my silky hair open.

There is no doubt that I looked dashing, and my husband never hesitates to compliment or steal a look.

Everything seemed okay until we stepped out and reached the mall.

We had driven to the mall, and I was already hungry.

We started to walk around, looking at the new things that were in the mall.

We then shopped for a few of the items on our list.

It was our usual end-of-the-month shopping that we did on the last Saturday of the month.

But before that, we wanted to grab a quick bite, so we all sat down at the food court.

As usual, my husband asked the boss of the house.

*"What do you want?"*

*"Maybe a burger from Mac,"* I said quietly, almost under my breath.

*"Alright, I will order through the app,"* he said instantly, like it was the easiest thing in the world.

*"Hmmm… okay,"* I responded, but my voice carried an unpleasant edge, one I didn't intend but couldn't hide.

*"What happened, you want something else?"* he asked me in a concerned tone, his eyebrows narrowing slightly as he studied my face.

*"No... it's fine. Let's get burgers for everyone, and after eating, let's get moving,"* I told him, trying to sound neutral but failing miserably.

*"You don't sound good,"* he said, looking at me, his eyes soft but filled with quiet questions.

---

He had no idea what was going on,
but he sensed something was wrong.

---

He was likely trying to figure out what had happened.

He looked at my face with an expression that said, *what did I miss?*

He started to wonder about all the things he possibly could have done wrong.

*"Did I say something wrong?"*

*"Did you want to go to the shop and then eat?"*

*"Did you want food before we started shopping?"*

He started to think aloud, fumbling for clues.

My heart was feeling heavy.

I did not feel good—this feeling I cannot explain.

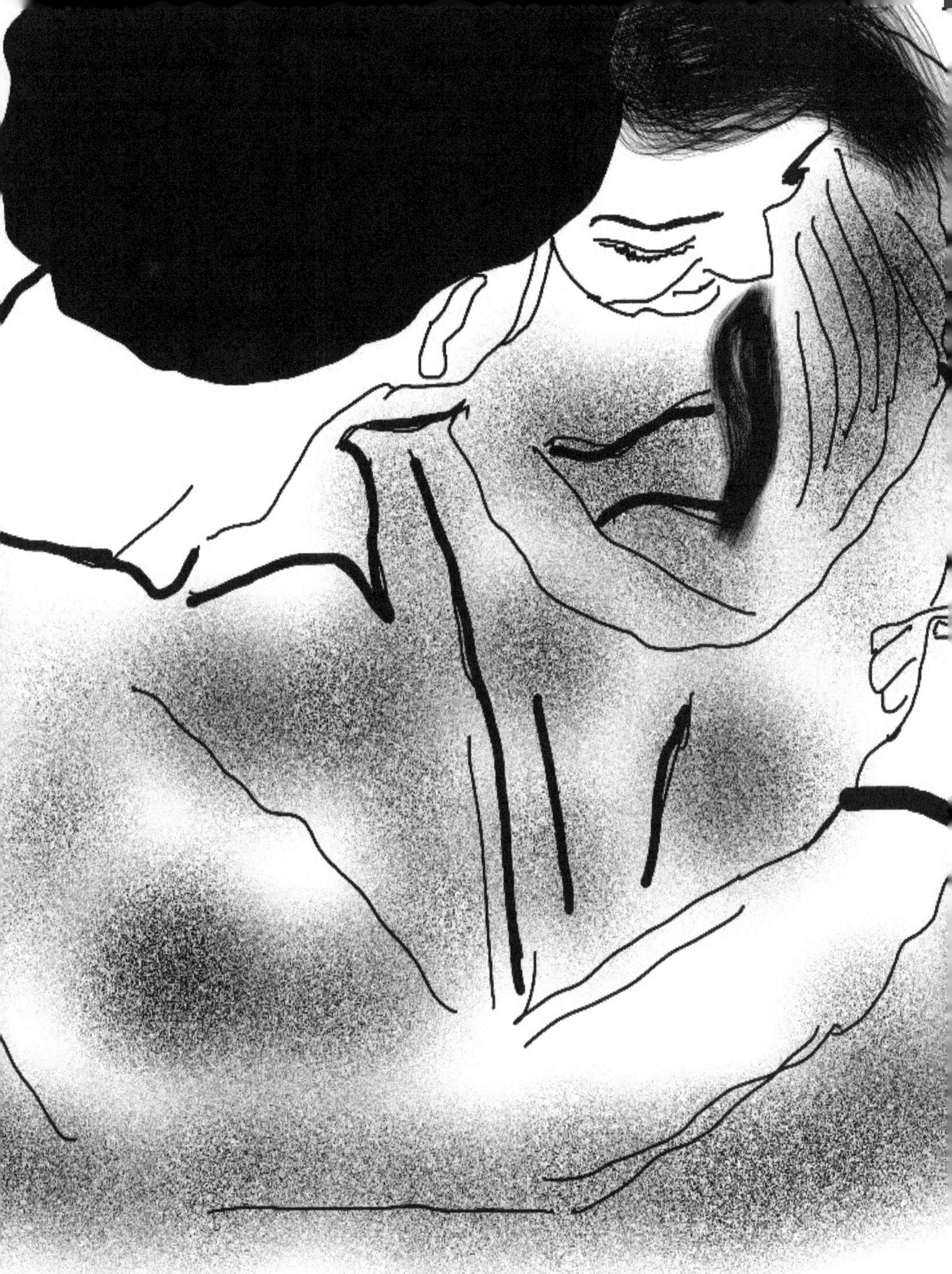

A feeling of being *little* and helpless and full of
shame.

My kids were happy and jumping at the thought of having food from outside, their laughter almost painful in contrast to the silence inside me.

He was trying to get the order done, but my behaviour was making him panic.

*"App's not working. Are you very hungry? Shall we order something else?"* He looked at me and spoke kindly, carefully, like he was afraid I would break.

I could see him trying his best to calm me.

---

I say *calm me* because, even though I was not shouting or yelling or saying anything in anger, my family could sense the fire in me— the invisible one, the quiet one that makes everyone around cautious.

---

My oldest one started saying jokes to bring a smile to my sad-struck face,

with me finally snapping and asking her to shut up.

*"Let's move out from here,"* I said and walked into the next café, with my family following me like a silent little parade.

We sat there, and I recollected that my children had told me that they wanted milkshakes and desserts.

*"Kids, buy whatever you want,"* I said to my children, my voice stiff and detached.

---

They bought whatever they wanted without any hesitation. No ego, only happiness and joy at what they were receiving.

---

When they were buying, I did not look at them or even budge from my seat.

My body felt nailed to the chair, my eyes fixed on nothing in particular.

My husband bought a vanilla cheesecake and said softly, *"You love this, right?"*

*"No, I don't want it,"* I said in a stern voice, sharper than I intended.

*"Come on, have something,"* he insisted, gently pushing the plate towards me.

*"No, I don't want to have anything,"* I told him again, my jaw tight.

He reminded me that I said I was hungry while I was in the car.

*"I am ok now; I don't want any food,"* I told him, almost shouting.

I felt very stiff, my whole body felt that way.

It was hard and unmovable.

It was behaving like just a structure with no soul inside.

My ego was killing me.

I felt like my system had collapsed from holding something up and couldn't hold it any longer.

I thought I might just die.

So, I closed my eyes for what must have been only ten seconds.

But in that little time, something miraculous happened.

---

An experience that took me to a higher plane of consciousness.

---

It was exceptional, uplifting, and freeing—like my soul had briefly stepped out of its usual cage and into the open sky.

In that fleeting instant, I had a vivid vision.

I saw Buddha, calm and serene, his eyes soft yet piercingly aware, walking barefoot and seeking alms at the door of a humble clay-walled home.

A woman stood there, simple clothes draped loosely around her, holding a small bowl of food. She offered it to him with lowered eyes and a shy, reverent smile.

Buddha accepted gently, cupping the bowl as though it was the most sacred offering in the world, and smiled—a smile so light and compassionate that it seemed to ripple through time.

Then he turned to me and said, his voice neither loud nor soft but *unshakably clear*:

*"Amy, crush your ego. That's your path to everything.*

*If you don't receive what you get freely from the loving people around you, one day you may have to be on your knees, put forth your hand to receive it from the people you don't even know.*

*So, crush that ego now. Be free and enjoy."*

The clarity of his words struck deep, echoing in my chest like a bell in a silent temple.

It wasn't just a message; it felt like a profound revelation—a reminder that the key to inner peace and fulfillment lies in letting go of the ego that binds us so tightly.

It was as if the vision had been sent deliberately, showing me the way forward on my personal journey.

I opened my eyes slowly, the world around me feeling strangely new, as if it had been gently dusted clean.

I reached for the spoon lying in front of me and took a bite of the cheesecake my husband had offered me earlier. The creamy sweetness filled my mouth, warm and grounding, pulling me back fully into the moment. Then, without hesitation, I asked for a share of my daughter's sandwich, and she happily offered me a piece.

---

My husband looked surprised. There I was, moments ago, an angry tiger, stiff and untouchable and now calm, soft, even smiling.

---

But all that mattered to him was that I was fine.

He watched me closely, peering a few times to check if this sudden calm was real, his face still laced with concern but softening with relief.

Suddenly, a gentle hand touched my shoulder.

*"Would you like to have some chocolates?"* It was the owner of the café, smiling brightly.

---

I was taken aback and asked him what the occasion was. *"Just a warm gesture from us, that's all,"* he said, placing a plate piled with assorted chocolates on our table.

---

We took a few, but he insisted we take more, almost playful in his generosity.

This time, I did not hesitate.

I reached out freely, gratefully, receiving it like a gift from the universe itself.

We enjoyed what we had bought at the café and then moved to another place for a proper lunch.

When I ordered a soup, the lady behind the counter smiled warmly and asked,

*"Would you like some sweets?"*

I nodded, and she handed me a small packet of sweets as though it were the most natural thing in the world.

I took it and thanked her with a broad smile that I felt from my chest rather than just my lips.

Something inside me loosened—something that had been tight and rigid for so long.

I felt... lighter.

The binding that had gripped me for years seemed to be untying itself, thread by stubborn thread.

My chest expanded more freely, and I could look at people and genuinely smile, truly *see* them, and be part of everything around me instead of apart from it.

---

As I walked with that tray of soup towards my loving family — my husband watching me with that soft, protective gaze and my kids beaming with relief at my smile.

---

I thought, 'What's my worth? I still don't know.

*But what I know now is that, if I want to understand, I should be willing...*

*Willing to break.*

*Willing to conquer.*

*And willing to crush, that untameable, gigantic ego of mine.'*

There is no doubt that it is hard to crush an ego even when it is crushing you from within. But what if it is this ego that is stopping you from being truly you and achieving everything that you ever wanted.

This short story **'CRUSH'** is dedicated to the painful hearts who cannot let go of that deceptive ego and suffers from sad and depressive thoughts.

May you be guided.

# Rose Butterfly

**Hi Readers & Thinkers**

My Warm Greetings!

The stories I've gathered in this book are incredibly dear to me, and each one was written with care. They are a blend of experiences, unspoken feelings, and indescribable emotions that sometimes people go through but are so delicate and therefore hardly confronted.

These emotions have many layers, and without realizing it may have caused a stir in our hearts.

To keep writing, I need your encouragement and support. If you enjoyed what you read, please leave a review to help others discover the book as well.

Feel free to share the stories with your friends, so they too can reflect, enjoy, and be moved by them. I'd love to hear from you, so don't hesitate to reach out. Your feedback will let me know that these stories have found their way into your heart.

Thanks & Love

Rose Butterfly

www.rosebutterfly.com.au

## About The Author

Rose Butterfly is a pen name of Deena Philip, an Australian writer and publisher, best known for her profoundly empathetic self-help guide, *The Book I Never Had*.

The book helps navigate heartbreaks and the lingering emotions of past relationships, providing readers with practical guidance. The work has resonated with many due to its relatable and understanding approach to emotional healing. She has also published a second edition to further answer her readers' questions.

Her work spans across different genres, and her versatile writing caters to both children and adults. She holds a Degree in Media & Communications and Psychology, and her work reflects a deep understanding of minds, relationships, philosophy and the human experience. She is also a theatre performer and an artist.

Her teen novel, *Laser Boy and Ice Girl*, is a thrilling sci-fi superhero comedy series for teens, while the *Izzy and Mia* collection, is a light and fun chapter book for younger readers.

*Heart-Stirring Moments* is a collection of short, introspective stories of life, its nuances, and moments. *Imperfect Minds* is volume two of the same collection.

Deena is also the head of the production house 'Cheer,' which is involved in multiple creative projects.

*www. cheerproductions.com.au*

*Visit the website to know more about the Author and other works.*

*www. rosebutterfly.com.au*

*Follow the Rose Butterfly Page on Facebook*

'Imperfect Minds' by Rose Butterfly is a collection of short stories that invites you to step beyond the visible elements of life and form a new understanding of perceptions, feelings, and relationships.

Although these tales explore **paradoxical, unconventional, paranormal, mind-bending and psychological** themes, at their core, they are all transcending moments.

**Available for purchase on Amazon.**

Enjoy this action-packed sci-fi comedy, **'Laser Boy &
Ice Girl- Volume 1 & 2.'** It is the ultimate genre
mashup, blending action, humour, and suspense into
Kapow-worthy moments that you wouldn't want to
miss.

- Perfect read for tweens and teens.
- Perfect choice for lovers of space and science
  fiction.
- Perfect book for comedy connoisseurs.

**Available for purchase on Amazon.**

# Quotes

## THE BOOK I NEVER HAD

Not accepting where you truly are will not only keep you in a loop of an illusion of moving forward.

But it will also restrain you from receiving life in its intended glory.

One cannot say, 'I let go' and assume that everything has moved away.

One of the key elements required in letting go is in establishing the understanding of 'why letting go is the right step for you.'

A compromised life,

An unfulfilled expectation from your partner can lead you into a space of belief that you are only worthy of so much.

If you are someone who have become comfortable where you are, by holding on to the bits and crumbs you get from life and have been continuing to live on this manner for some time, but still complaining that you are not able to move on, you need to ask yourself what exactly are you doing?

What do you want?

We unbelievably have the full capacity to go wrong about the closest people, the people we call love or the people we have high expectations from.

You are not here to live and set another example of
a told tale, you are here to live yours.

No one can make those life-changing decisions for you. You need to do it yourself.

Be honest about your situation and have the openness to receive something better.

Consistently experiencing the feeling of being stuck will only allow you to grow and flourish in that space.

At this point it is very important that you change your focus to something else, even if you are able to do it only for a very short time.

If you do not reclaim into being a whole person, you are not going to be happy and finding somebody can never bring the true happiness that you are seeking.

# Thank you

My most sincere thanks to my family for supporting me in this crazy journey.

Thank you for loving me so much and allowing me to be whoever I am.

I know I can be difficult at times, and I really appreciate your warmth and understanding.

I hope that you all will continue to be the same.

I promise I will.